English language edition published exclusively by
C.D. Stampley Enterprises, Inc.
Charlotte, NC USA
www.stampley.com

Artwork and concept by
Creations for Children International, Belgium.
www.c4ci.com
Illustrations by P. Gayen, R. Das, P. Kohli

ISBN 1-58087-100-3
Stampley code number B113

Printed in China – 2005

BILLY & BAXTER™

At the AIRPORT

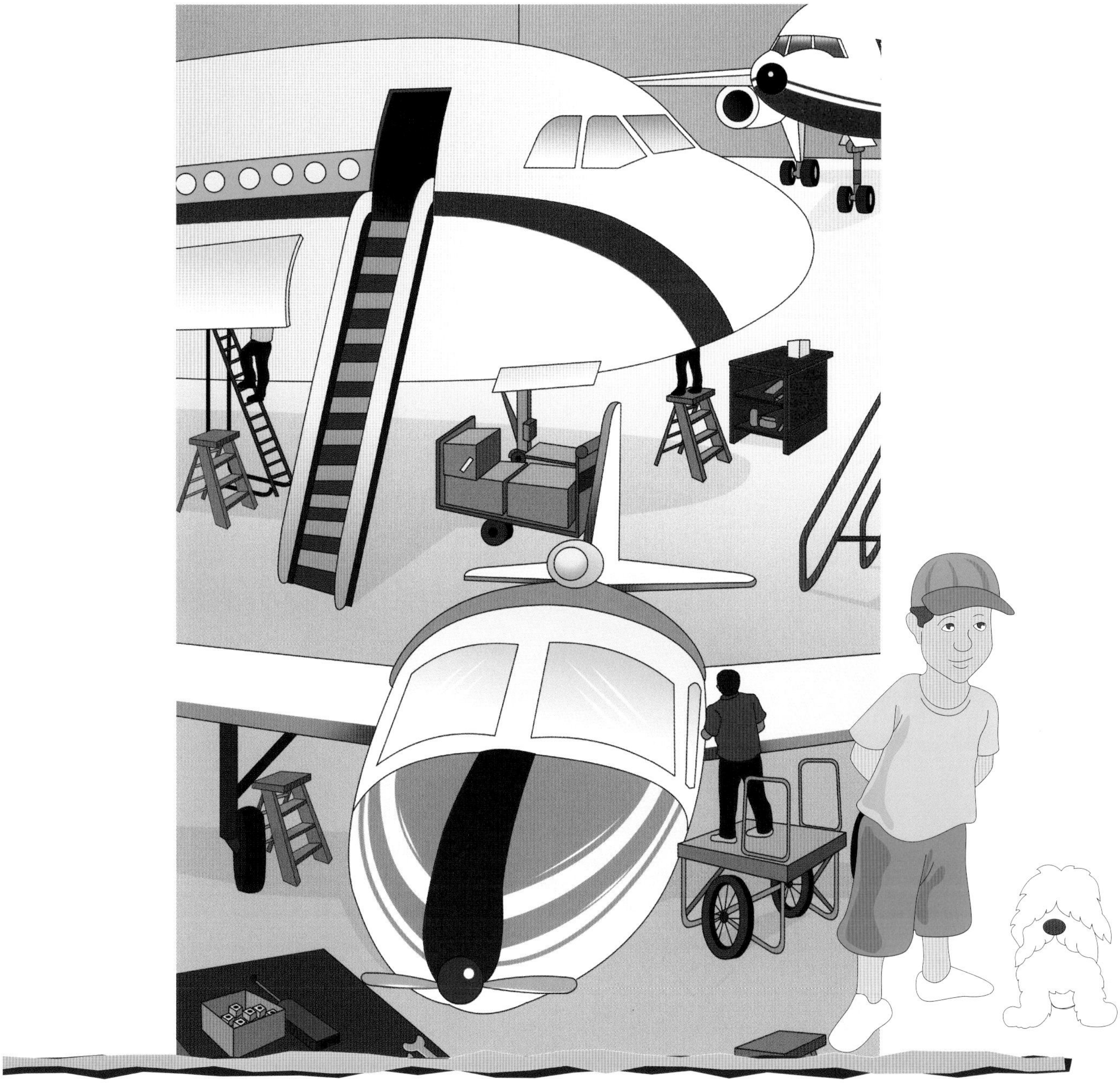

STAMPLEY

Entrance

Billy and Baxter are at the airport. The terminal building is huge. There are many people traveling, and lots of cars and buses. Uncle Joe works at the airport. He repairs airplanes.

CAR RENTAL
TAXIS

Terminal building

Inside the airport there are many things to do — ride the escalator, buy snacks and shop for souvenirs. Then you go to the gate, board the airplane and you are on your way!

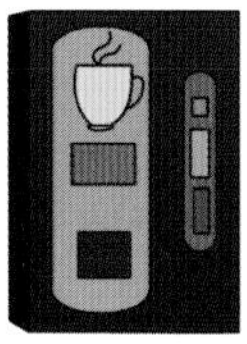
coffee vending machine

directions

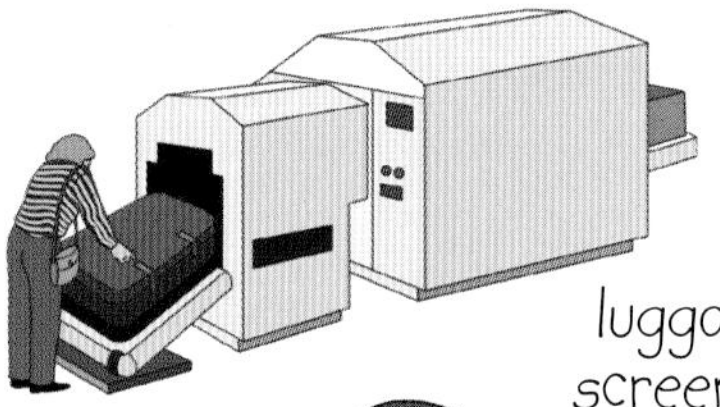
luggage screening

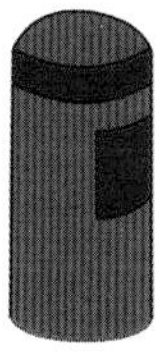
trash can

clock

automatic teller machine (ATM)

souvenirs

information

backpack

escalator

INFORMATION
COFFEE SHOP
SHOPS
LUGGAGE SCREENING
SHUTTLE SERVICE
RESTROOMS
EXIT
ATM

Check-in

At the check-in counter passengers' tickets and passports are reviewed. Billy has fun watching all the luggage as it rides the conveyor belt. Soon it will be loaded onto an airplane.

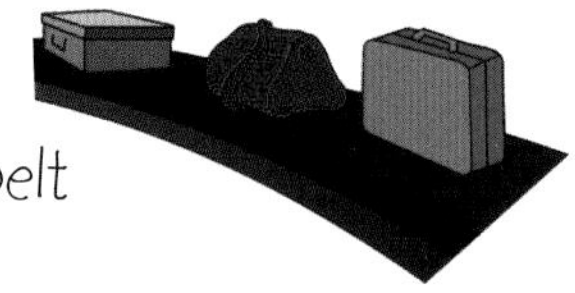

conveyor belt

coffee shop

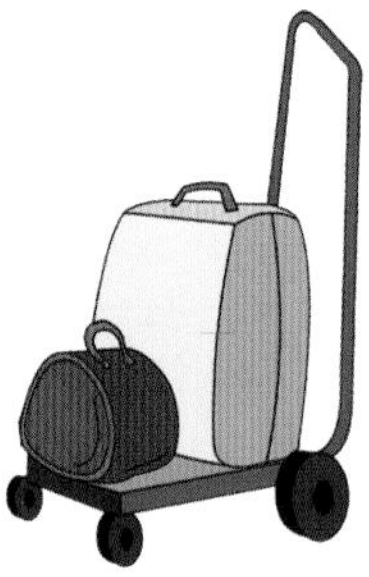

carry-on luggage

luggage cart

restrooms

No Smoking sign

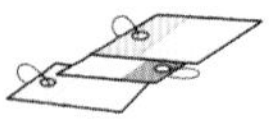

luggage tags

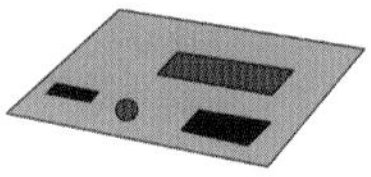

luggage weight display

tickets and passport

ticket agent

CHECK-IN
PASSPORT CONTROL

At the gate

Passengers wait for flights in the boarding area. But first they must pass through a metal detector. All carry-on luggage is checked by security officers. Where is Baxter?

security officer

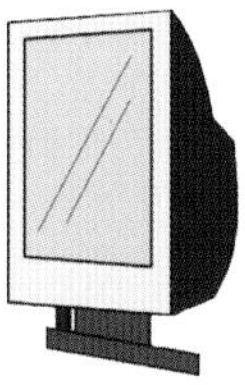

television

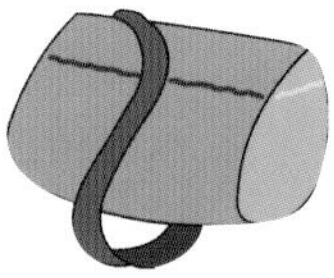

duffel bag

waiting chair

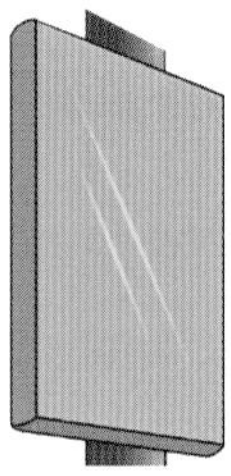

information screen

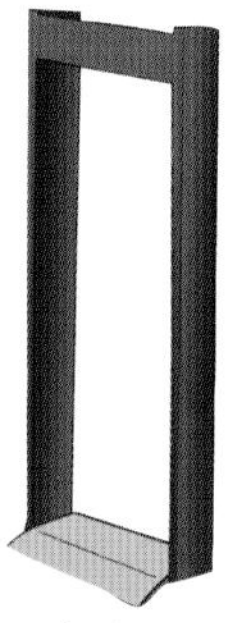

metal detector

X-ray monitor

briefcase

sign

luggage screener

GATE-1
GATE-2
GATE-3
TERMINAL-1
TERMINAL-2

Maintenance

Airplanes must be carefully maintained. A cleaning crew washes the airplane. Another crew loads cargo, while another pumps fuel. Billy and Baxter just watch.

On the tarmac

Passengers sometimes climb boarding stairs to enter an airplane. A flight attendant greets each person at the door. With everyone safely on board workers remove the stairs.

The hangar

Uncle Joe is an airplane mechanic. In the hangar area Billy and Baxter see engineers and mechanics working to keep the planes safe. How lucky to see an airplane inside and out, from cockpit to tail!

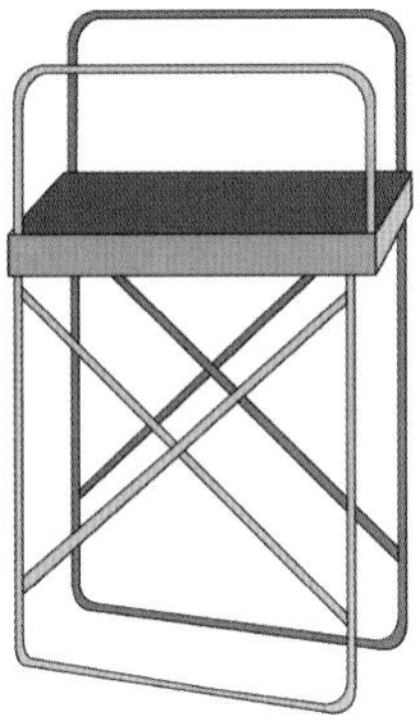

working platform

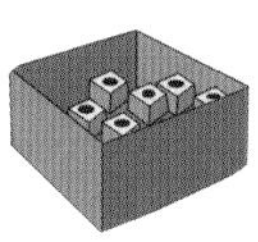

nuts & bolts

wrenches

hammer

engineer

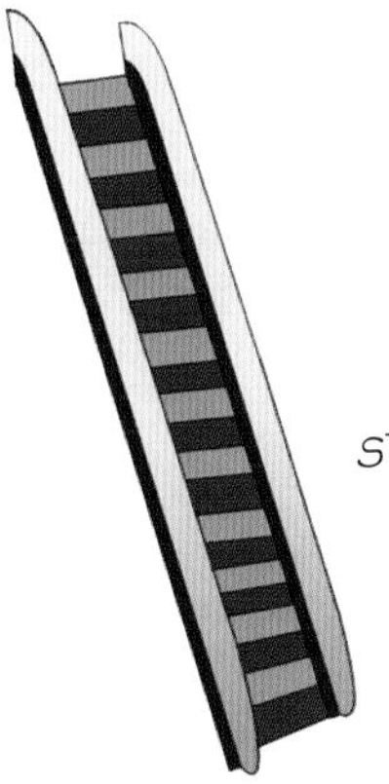

stairs

stool

jet engine

fuselage

wing

Glossary

automatic teller machine (ATM) — a machine that gives out money from a person's bank account

boarding stairs — a special staircase on wheels that passengers use to enter and exit an airplane

cargo — goods carried by an airplane, ship, truck or train

cockpit — the front of the airplane where the pilot sits and controls the flight

conveyor belt — a long moving belt that takes things from one place to another

crosswalk — a path where people may safely cross a street

engineer — a person who is trained to build and operate machines and engines

escalator — a moving staircase

flight attendant — a person who cares for passengers on an airplane

fuel tanker — a truck that carries fuel, like gas or oil

fuselage — the main body of an airplane

hangar — a large shed used to repair and store airplanes

mechanic — a person who repairs machines

metal detector — a machine that gives a signal when something made of metal passes through it

passenger — a person who travels in a vehicle, such as a car or plane

passport — the official papers that prove who a person is and allow him to travel to other countries

pilot — a person who is trained to fly an airplane

shuttle bus — a bus that carries people for a short distance, like from the terminal to the plane

skycap — a person at the airport who helps you with your luggage

tarmac — an airport runway made of stone and tar

wings — the two "arms" that stick off the sides of an airplane to help it fly (like the wings of a bird)